W9-AVE-472

No Sit-Ups for Porky Pig

by GINA INGOGLIA
illustrated by JOE MESSERLI

A GOLDEN BOOK • NEW YORK
Western Publishing Company, Inc., Racine, Wisconsin 53404

Copyright © 1985 by Warner Bros. Inc. All rights reserved. Printed in the U.S.A. by Western Publishing Company, Inc. No part of this book may be reproduced or copied in any form without written permission from the publisher. PORKY PIG is the trademark of Warner Bros. Inc. used under license. GOLDEN®, GOLDEN & DESIGN®, A GOLDEN TELL-A-TALE® BOOK, and A GOLDEN BOOK® are trademarks of Western Publishing Company, Inc. Library of Congress Catalog Card Number: 85-70333   ISBN 0-307-07009-3

MCMXCI

"Hi, Cicero," said Petunia Pig. "Is your Uncle Porky at home?"

"Sure," said Cicero. "Come on in."

"Porky," said Petunia, "please join our jogging club. You're really out of shape."

"I'm in great shape," Porky Pig said, between bites.

"Petunia, show Porky how you can do sit-ups," said Cicero.

"All right," said Petunia Pig.

"One, two, three, four, five," counted Cicero. "Five sit-ups for Petunia!"

"Anyone can do that," said Porky. He got down on the floor, but couldn't budge.

"Zero," counted Cicero. "No sit-ups for Porky!"

"Maybe he can touch his toes," sighed Petunia.

"That's easy," said Porky Pig, bending over.
"How's this?" he gasped.

"Not very good, Uncle Porky," said Cicero.
"You're touching your knees, not your toes."

"I've had enough of this," said Porky, heading for the kitchen.

"He has to exercise more," said Petunia.

"Don't worry," said Cicero. "I'll think of something."

The doorbell rang. It was the jogging club.

"Porky," said Bugs Bunny, "are you coming?"

"I've already exercised with Petunia," said Porky.

"Doc," said Bugs, "you eat too much."

"I never eat too much," said Porky.

"He means," said Petunia, "that he can never eat enough."

"Are you weady to go?" asked Elmer Fudd.
Cicero whispered to Petunia. "Go jogging
without me. I've thought of a way to make Uncle
Porky move!"

As soon as the joggers left, Porky Pig sat down. "I think I'll take a little nap," he said.

Cicero hid behind the stairs.

"Uncle Porky!" he shouted. "Come look at what I found upstairs!"

Porky ran upstairs.

"Where are you, Cicero?" he called.

"I'm downstairs!" answered Cicero.

Porky ran downstairs.
"Where are you, Cicero?" he called.
"I'm outside!" answered Cicero.

Porky ran outside. He ran around to the back of the house.

"Hi, Uncle Porky," said Cicero. "Now I'm inside!"

Porky Pig was very annoyed.

"What's all this upstairs, downstairs, outside, inside business?" he asked.

"I promised Petunia I'd get you to move," said Cicero. "And I did!"

The jogging club raced over to Porky and
Cicero.

"Is anything wrong?" asked Daffy Duck. "We
saw you running, Porky."

"Cicero got me to run," said Porky. "And it
really felt good."

"Great!" said Bugs. "Now you can join us!"

"Wait for me!" said Cicero, dashing out of the house.

"Let's go!" said Petunia.
She led the jogging club down the street with
their newest member—Porky Pig!